Sleep Tight, Charlie

Michaël Escoffier

Kris Di Giacomo

Peachtree

After a busy day,
Charlie gets ready for bed.

He places a glass of water
on his bedside table.

He puts his slippers on the rug.

He makes sure there isn't
a monster under his bed.

He hugs his
teddy bear tight.

He closes one eye,
then the other.

And then Charlie falls asleep.

TAP TAP TAP TAP TAP TAP

PTAP
APTAP
TAPTAP
TAP

Charlie awakes with a **start**.

What **is** that racket?

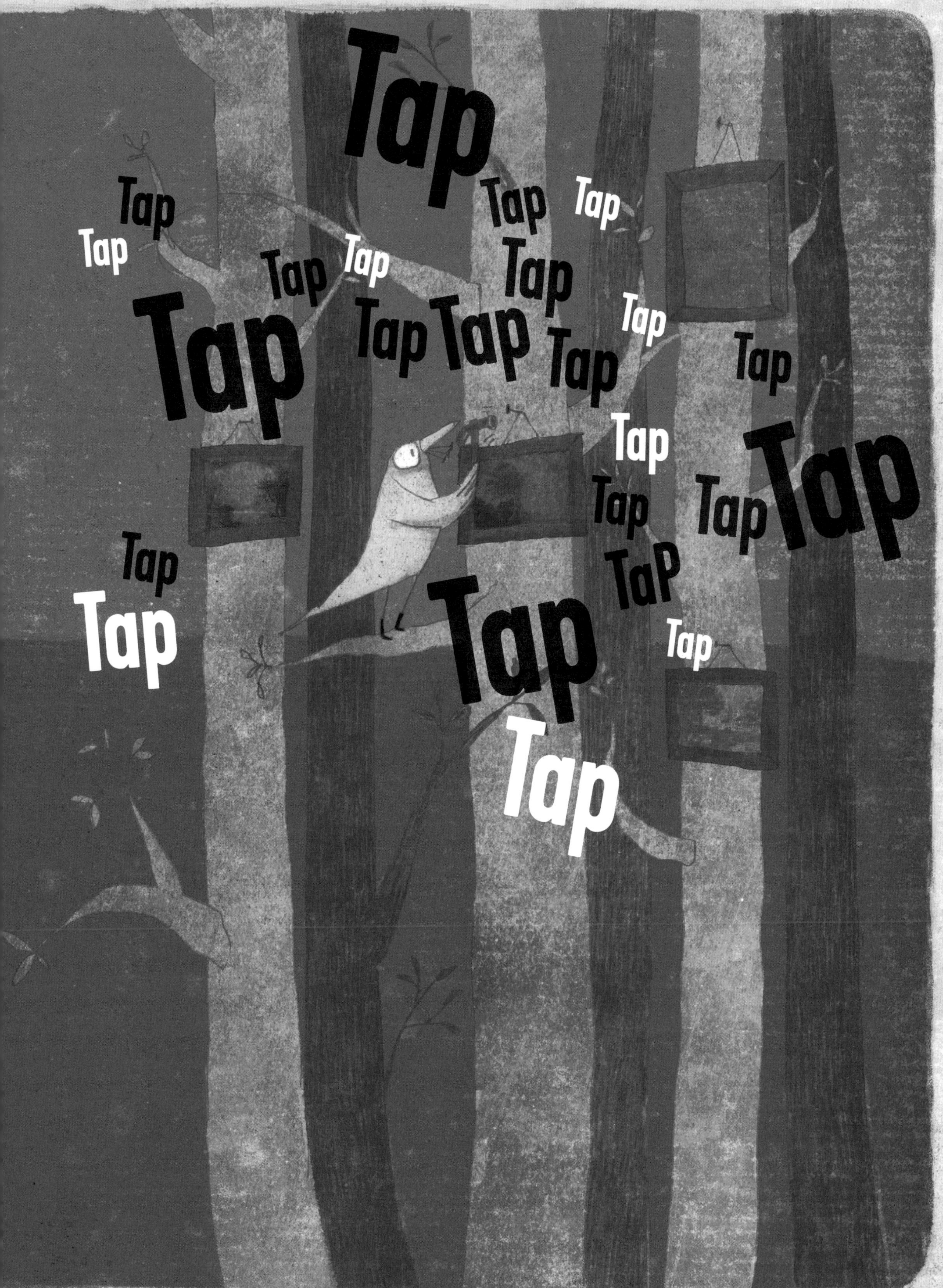
Tap
Tap
Tap
Tap
Tap
Tap
Tap
Tap
Tap
Tap
Tap
Tap
Tap
Tap
Tap
Tap
Tap
Tap
Tap
TaP
Tap
Tap
Tap
Tap

"Pardon me, Bird,
do you know what time it is?"

"Sorry, I thought I was alone out here."

"Well, you're not, and it's bedtime.
I am trying to **sleep!**"

"No problem,"

says Bird, and he flies away.

Back at home...

Charlie drinks a sip of water.

He places his glass back
on his bedside table.

He puts his slippers on the rug.

He makes sure there isn't
a monster under his bed.

He hugs his teddy bear tight.

He closes one eye, then the other.

And then Charlie falls asleep.

Crunch!
Crunch!
Crunch!

Crunch!

Crunch!

Crunch!

Charlie is wide awake.

"Excuse me, Squirrel, are you planning to crack nuts **all night?**"

"Winter is coming. I need food!"

crunch

crunch

crunch

crunch

crunch

crunch

"Winter is **six months away!**
Don't you think it's a bit early?"

"It's never too early."

"You're right. It's never too early—
to sleep! Now, knock it off!"

Back at home...

Charlie empties his glass
of water.

He places his teddy bear
on his bedside table.

He makes sure there isn't
a monster under the rug.

He hugs his slippers tight.

He closes one eye,
then the other.

And then Charlie falls asleep.

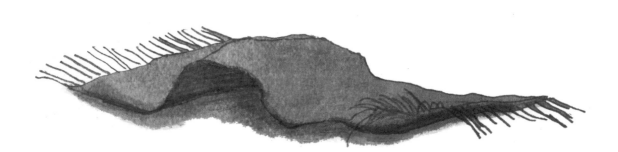

Squeeeeak!

Squeeeeeak

Squee

Charlie is awake again.

"Hey, Mouse!
What is this ruckus?
It's too late to play on the swings!
And you'd better watch out—
the big cats come out at night!"

Charlie can finally sleep.

He puts his slippers in his empty glass.

He makes sure there isn't a teddy bear in the bedside table.

He hugs his rug tight.

He closes one eye, then the other.

And then Charlie falls asleep.

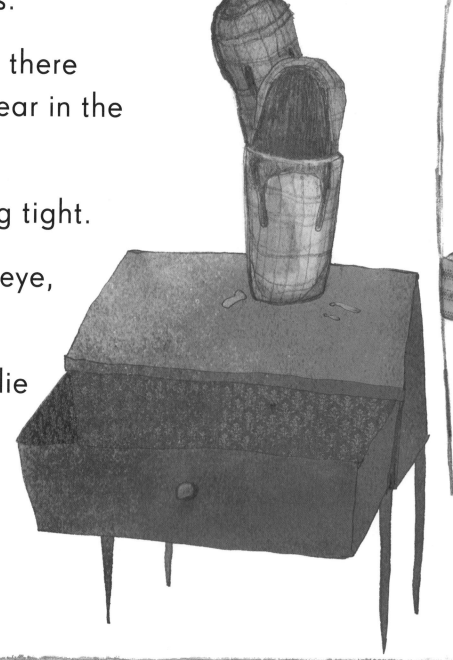

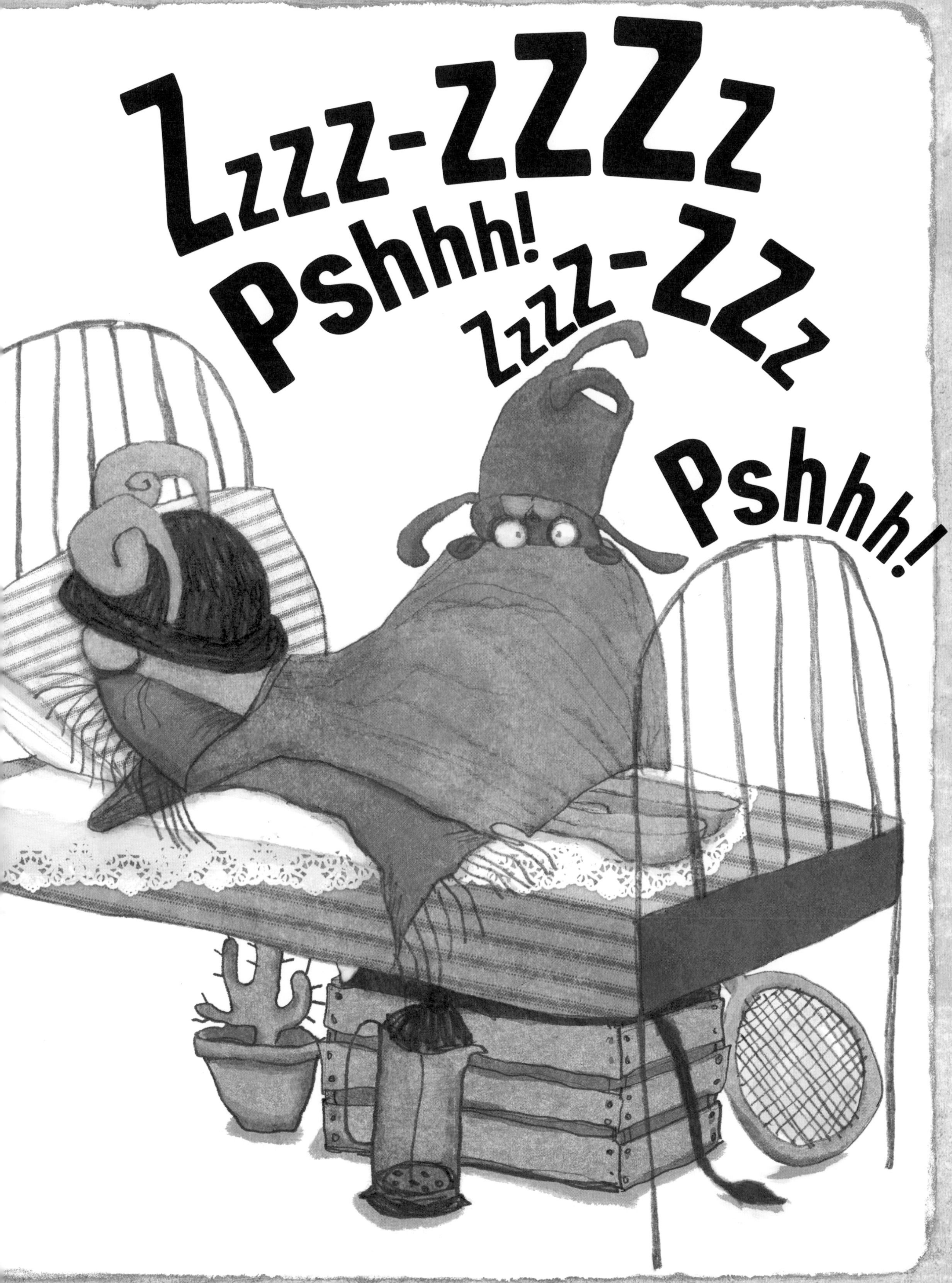
Zzzz-zZZZz
Pshhh!
Zzzz-ZZz
Pshhh!

BANG!

BAN

NG!
BANG!